Mama's Milk Is All Gone

Written by Ann P Vernon
Illustrated by LeeAnn Gorman

To my June,
thank you for expanding
my understanding of LOVE.

When I was born
Mama held me close
and fed me from her body.

Mama's milk helped me
grow big and strong.

I grew . . .

and grew . . .

and grew . . .

. . .and grew.

Mama still loves
to hold me close,
even though Mama's
milk is all gone.

I know Mama loves me.

If I am feeling sad,
I get lots of hugs and kisses
to help me feel better.

I know Mama loves me.

If I am hungry we make wonderful healthy foods to fill my belly.

I know Mama loves me.

If I am thirsty,
she gives me water to drink.

I know Mama loves me.

If I am tired
I cuddle up
and close my eyes.

I have wonderful memories of Mama feeding me milk from her body.

Now we make new memories in many different ways.

We read together.

We dance together.

We learn together.

We build together.

We explore together.

We sing together.

We create together.

We grow together.

Sometimes I miss Mama's Milk.
But when Mama hugs me
and holds me tight
I remember all the ways
we share our love.

Made in the USA
Middletown, DE
24 July 2022

69948593R00020